Kylie Jean

Soccer Queen

by Marci Peschke

illustrated by Tuesday Mourning

PICTURE WINDOW BOOKS

a capstone imprint

Kylie Jean is published by Picture Window Books
A Capstone Imprint
1710 Roe Crest Drive
North Mankato, Minnesota 56003
www.capstoneyoungreaders.com

Library of Congress Cataloging-in-Publication Data

Peschke, M. (Marci), author.
  Soccer queen / by Marci Pescke ; illustrated by Tuesday Mourning.
    pages cm. — (Kylie Jean)
Summary: After watching a soccer game, Kylie Jean is eager to try out for a local team, but she is disappointed that her cousin Lucy does not want to join her.
  ISBN 978-1-4795-5882-7 (hardcover) — ISBN 978-1-4795-5884-1 (paper over board) —
  ISBN 978-1-4795-6199-5 (eBook PDF) — ISBN 978-1-4795-6172-8 (paperback)
1. Soccer stories. 2. Cousins—Juvenile fiction. 3. Friendship—Juvenile fiction. 4. Families—Texas—Juvenile fiction. 5. Texas—Juvenile fiction. [1. Soccer—Fiction. 2. Cousins—Fiction. 3. Friendship—Fiction. 4. Family life—Texas—Fiction. 5. Texas—Fiction.] I. Mourning, Tuesday, illustrator. II. Title. III. Series: Peschke, M. (Marci) Kylie Jean.
  PZ7.P441245So 2015
  813.6—dc23

                          2014022720

Graphic Designer: *Kristi Carlson*

Editor: *Alison Deering*

Production Specialist: *Laura Manthe*

Design Element Credit:
Shutterstock/blue67design

Printed and bound in China.
012017   010216R

For Poppie and Grandpa Bob
—MP

Table of Contents

All About Me, Kylie Jean!

My name is Kylie Jean Carter. I live in a big, sunny, yellow house on Peachtree Lane in Jacksonville, Texas, with Momma, Daddy, and my two brothers, T.J. and Ugly Brother.

T.J. is my older brother, and Ugly Brother is . . . well . . . he's really a dog. Don't you go telling him he is a dog. Okay? I mean it. He thinks he is a real, true person.

He is a black-and-white bulldog. His front looks like his back, all smashed in. His face is all droopy like he's sad, but he's not.

His two front teeth stick out, and his tongue hangs down. (Now you know why his name is Ugly Brother.)

Everyone I love to the moon and back lives in Jacksonville. Nanny, Pa, Granny, Pappy, my aunts, my uncles, and my cousins all live here. I'm extra lucky, because I can see all of them any time I want to!

My momma says I'm pretty. She says I have eyes as blue as the summer sky and a smile as sweet as an angel. (Momma says pretty is as pretty does. That means being nice to the old folks, taking care of little animals, and respecting my momma and daddy.)

But I'm pretty on the outside and on the inside. My hair is long, brown, and curly.

I wear it in a ponytail sometimes, but my absolute most favorite is when Momma pulls it back in a princess style on special days.

I just gave you a little hint about my big dream. Ever since I was a bitty baby I have wanted to be an honest-to-goodness beauty queen. I even know the wave. It's side to side, nice and slow, with a dazzling smile. I practice all the time, because everybody knows beauty queens need to have a perfect wave.

I'm Kylie Jean, and I'm going to be a beauty queen. Just you wait and see!

Chapter 1
Benbrook Buccaneers

When I wake up, it is a perfect Saturday morning. It's springtime, and the sky is as blue as a robin's egg, with just a few wispy white clouds. The breeze is blowing, and the birds are singing. Miss Clarabelle, my next-door neighbor, would call it glorious.

The best part of this Saturday morning is that Momma has a surprise for me! All week long I have been trying to figure out what her mysterious surprise is. I've tried guessing, begging, and snooping, but I still can't figure it out!

As soon as I am awake, I run downstairs and see that Momma has a big Saturday morning breakfast waiting. She even made my favorite blueberry pancakes. Yum! She also made Ugly Brother's favorite maple bacon. Ruff, ruff! I take a seat at the kitchen table and dig in.

"How are those pancakes?" Momma asks me.

"They are the most delicious pancakes in the whole wide world!" I reply.

Momma laughs. "Thank you," she says, "but if you think your sweet compliments are going to make me tell you about my surprise, they're not! You'll just have to wait and see!"

"Buttering you up seemed like a good plan to me, and I just had to try one more time to find out what it is," I say.

My older brother T.J. is busy shoveling pancakes in his mouth. Between bites, he mumbles, "Got lawns to mow today."

"Don't forget to check with Miss Clarabelle and ask about mowing her lawn too," Momma tells him.

T.J. mumbles again with his mouth full, which probably means okay.

"Kylie Jean, you'd better wash the syrup off your hands and face," Momma says. "It's almost time to go."

"Go where?" I ask.

But Momma just shakes her head. "It's a surprise," she reminds me.

Once I am cleaned up, I wait by the front door while Momma gets her purse. When she comes toward me, I spy a clue. She has her game bag! Whenever T.J. has sports games, Momma brings a bag with sunscreen, water, snacks, a magazine, and a first aid kit. We must be going to a game!

But wait a second . . . T.J. is mowing lawns today, not playing sports. Hmm . . . this is very curious.

"Come on, Ugly Brother!" Momma calls, holding out his leash. This must be a clue too! I bet we're going to a doggie-friendly place.

Finally it's time to go. We hop in Momma's van, and I watch the road, trying to see which way we are turning. Maybe I can figure out where we are headed.

Before long I recognize the road we're on. "I know!" I holler. "We're going to Lucy's house!"

Momma smiles. "We are, but only because Lucy is going to join us for the surprise," she tells me. She stops in my cousin Lucy's driveway and honks. *Beep, beep!* Lucy runs out and hops in the van beside me.

"Don't forget to buckle your seat belt," Momma reminds her from the front seat.

Lucy looks as excited as I feel. "Where are we going?" she asks.

I shrug. "I can't figure it out, and Momma won't tell me!"

Before long we are turning into the parking lot of our community college. The sign in front of the school says, "Go, Buccaneers!"

Finally Momma says, "The Benbrook College Buccaneers are playing a big soccer game today — and we're going to watch. Surprise!"

"Yay!" Lucy and I cheer. Ugly Brother chimes in, barking twice. We park, and Momma pulls a lawn chair out of the back of the van. Ugly Brother tries to scramble out.

"Sorry, Ugly Brother," Momma tells him, "but you'll have to wear your leash. The players would not like it if you ran out onto the field to chase the ball."

Ugly Brother is not too happy, but he sits down so Momma can hook the leash to his collar.

"You're a good sport," I tell him.

We cross the parking lot. Momma carries her chair, Lucy carries the game bag, and I hold Ugly Brother's leash. Anxious to see what is happening, he drags me ahead of Momma and Lucy. I am not walking him — he is walking me!

On the sidelines of the field, people are sitting on chairs and on the ground. We pick a spot and get settled. Lucy and I sit on the cool green grass. Ugly Brother sits beside us. Momma pulls snacks out of her bag: water and trail mix for us, and beef jerky for Ugly Brother.

After a few minutes, the players arrive, and we all cheer and clap as they run out onto the field. The girls in the black-and-purple uniforms are the Buccaneers. The other team, the Roadrunners, has red-and-yellow jerseys.

The game starts, and I am amazed by the players' fancy footwork. One player even uses her head to hit the ball! Every time the Roadrunners move the ball down the field, the goalie for the Buccaneers stops them from scoring. She is amazing!

I think the Buccaneers are going to win because the other team can't score any points. But then one of the Roadrunners' players kicks the ball into the net. Oh, no!

The game is fast-paced and exciting. I shout and point and cheer, "Come on, Buccaneers!" I look over at Lucy to see if she's having fun, but she seems a little bored.

Back on the field, one of the Buccaneers moves the ball down the field and scores again for our team. The buzzer sounds, and I look up at the scoreboard. It reads 1-5 Buccaneers — we won!

The crowd goes crazy! The players run around jumping up and down and hugging each other. Then they head over and shake hands with the losing team.

"What good sportsmanship," Momma says. "I think those players are good role models for you girls."

I see the girl who scored the most goals standing over on the sidelines. There is a long line of younger girls waiting to get her autograph. I hurry over and wait my turn. When I get to the front of the line, I introduce myself. "I'm Kylie Jean Carter, and I want to be a soccer queen just like you!"

"It's nice to meet you, Kylie Jean," the girl says. "I'm Belle Jenkins. You know, if you really want to be a soccer queen, you should join one of the rec center teams. I'm going to be one of the coaches."

"Oh, boy!" I exclaim. "I'm ready to sign up right now!"

Belle hands me a flier to give to Momma and explains that my parent has to do the paperwork. I run right over and tell Lucy everything I learned.

Lucy just pouts. "I want to go home," she says. "Soccer is boring."

I can hardly believe it. My best cousin and I do a lot together, but I think I'll be going to soccer camp on my own. Apparently Lucy does not want to be a soccer queen!

Chapter 2
A New Friend

That night I ask Momma to help me find soccer tryouts for our local rec center teams. "Please!" I beg. "Belle said I should sign up."

Momma smiles and says, "Okay, but it's too late to call. We'll just look up their tryout schedule on the Internet."

We sit at Momma's desk in the corner of the kitchen, and she turns on the computer. "I knew you'd love soccer!" she says.

I smile. "Momma, you know what I like before I do!"

Momma types in the website for the rec center. "This says they're holding tryouts Monday after school at the Jacksonville park. And a practice session tomorrow afternoon."

"That means tryouts are only two days away!" I exclaim. That's hardly any time at all for me to become a soccer queen!

I think quietly for a minute. "I want to try out, but I am feeling a little nervous. I think Lucy should come along too."

"That's a good idea," Momma agrees. "Maybe you should call Lucy and ask her to try out with you."

"Great idea!" I agree. I pick up the phone and dial Lucy's number. *Ring! Ring!*

"Hello," Lucy answers.

"Hey, it's me, Kylie Jean," I say. "Do you want to try out for the soccer team with me Monday after school?"

For a while it's as quiet as a church on Sunday. I wait and wait for Lucy to say something. Finally she says, "Hmm . . . I'll think on it and let you know tomorrow if I want to try out."

"Please think about saying yes!" I beg her. "You know we always make a great team!"

"I know," Lucy says.

We hang up, and I feel a little worried. Lucy doesn't seem very excited.

* * *

On Sunday after church, Momma takes me to the park so I can practice my footwork. When we arrive, I see lots of girls working on moving the ball around the soccer field with their feet. They make it look easy!

I know from reading on the rec center's website that what those girls are doing is called dribbling. You can't touch a soccer ball with your hands — it's against the rules!

Momma finds a spot on the sidelines to sit and read the book she brought with her, and I run to the field. I start dribbling the ball back and forth with another player. She has black hair and brown eyes and is wearing lots of stretchy, colorful bracelets.

We run up and down the field. The other girl seems like a really good soccer player. We are breathing hard from running so much, and my sweaty pink T-shirt is sticking to my back. Finally, I decide to take a break. "My name's Kylie Jean!" I say. "What's yours?"

"Ana Sofia!" she replies.

"I sure do like your bracelets," I tell her,
admiring them.

"Thanks," Ana Sofia says. "These two are my lucky ones." She points to a black one with soccer balls on it and a white one that says "#1 Player." "I got them after my very first soccer game."

Right then and there I decide I like Ana Sofia. She has two names just like me! She is so nice that I just know she'll be my new friend.

Suddenly I notice some coaches are watching us from the sidelines. I see Belle standing there too. "Tryouts aren't till tomorrow," I say. "I wonder what the coaches are doing here."

"They come to watch because it's easier to see what we can do if they see us play more than once," Ana Sofia says. "It's better for us too. If you mess up one day, you still have another chance."

I grin. "Second chances are fantastic!"

We are close to the goal, so I take a shot. The black-and-white ball flies right in! Ana Sofia gives me a high five. I sure hope Belle and the other coaches saw me score.

"You should be an attacker," Ana Sofia says. "They try to score. The coaches are always looking for attackers. We need defenders too. They keep the other team from scoring."

Just then, I hear Momma calling me. "Kylie Jean!" she hollers. "We need to get going so I can start supper!"

"Bye, Ana Sofia!" I say with a wave. "I sure hope we get to play on the same team."

"Me too!" Ana Sofia agrees. "See ya, Kylie Jean."

When we get home, I decide to practice some more. Luckily, Ugly Brother wants to play too, so I have a four-legged player on my team! He runs back and forth across the yard with me. He wants to be a soccer player too. Too bad they don't have doggie soccer teams!

Chapter 3
Soccer Tryouts

The next morning on the school bus, I sit by my best cousin Lucy. "Are you ready for tryouts?" I ask her.

Lucy shakes her head. "I don't think I want to play soccer," she says.

I am not surprised, but I'm as sad as a player without a team until I remember my new friend Ana Sofia. "You know what?" I say. "That's okay. Best cousins don't always have to do everything together."

Lucy smiles. "Yup!" she agrees. "We'll always be best cousins no matter what."

All day I think about trying out for the soccer team. My stomach does nonstop flip-flops, and I can hardly eat my lunch. After school Momma comes to pick me up so we can go to the soccer park.

When we get to the soccer field, Momma gives me a big squeezy hug. "Try not to be nervous," she says. "Just do your best. I'll be watching."

"Thanks, Momma," I reply.

There are a lot of girls there. I look left and right, searching for Ana Sofia. Finally I spy her standing beside Coach Belle and another coach and wave. Ana Sofia waves me over.

"Hi, Kylie Jean!" she says. "Do you know Coach Belle and Coach Kristy?"

"I know Coach Belle," I reply. I turn to the other coach and say, "It's nice to meet you."

"It's nice to meet you too, Kylie Jean," Coach Kristy replies.

Both coaches seem super nice, but I want to be on Coach Belle's team!

"Come on," Ana Sofia says. "I'll introduce you to some of the other girls."

We walk over to a group of players, and Ana Sofia introduces me to some of the girls she played with last year: Miranda, Layla, and Ava.

Just then Coach Belle calls, "Gather around, girls!" and we all hurry over to sit in a circle.

"I'm so glad to see so many faces at tryouts today," Coach Belle says, smiling at all of us. "Today we're going to do some drills and then have a scrimmage. That means we'll divide into teams and play against each other just like a regular game."

Coach Kristy continues, "Since we have so many girls wanting to play, we'll be playing several four-on-four scrimmages. Coach Belle and I will be watching to see how well you understand the game."

I lean over and whisper to Ana Sofia. "Now I am really worried. I've never played soccer before!"

"Have you watched very many games?" Ana Sofia whispers back.

"A few," I reply. "My brother T.J. is a soccer player."

"Just think about those games and watch me. You'll figure out what to do in no time," Ana Sofia says.

Before I know it, it's time to start the drills. First we have passing drills. Luckily Ana Sofia and I practiced passing yesterday, so I know what to do right away.

Next the coaches tell us it's time to work on dribbling. It's not too hard either. The whole time, the coaches watch us and make notes on their clipboards. I sure hope they think I'm doing a good job!

Soon we are all demonstrating what we know about shooting. I realize right away how lucky I was when I scored a goal yesterday. Shooting is harder than it looks! An older girl is playing goalie, and she is blocking all of our shots. Finally Ana Sofia manages to sneak one past her! I give her a high five.

The last thing the coaches ask us to do is juggle. They explain that in soccer, juggling means keeping the ball in the air using any part of your body except your hands. I'm not very good at it yet, but Ana Sofia is a pro. I'm going to ask her to give me some tips!

Soon it's time for the scrimmage. The coaches divide us into several teams of four. Ana Sofia is not on my team, but Ava is. She has red hair and lots of freckles. I like her because she's spunky.

"Stick with me," Ava says. "I'll help you."

I grin at her. "Thanks!"

My group is one of the last to scrimmage. We're going to be playing against Ana Sofia and Miranda. I've been carefully watching the other games so I can do my best. The coaches stand on the sidelines ready to take more notes. Then Coach Belle blows her whistle, and we're off!

The other team gets the ball right away, so we're on defense. Ava steals the ball and passes it to me. Miranda tries to stop me, but I dribble to our goal and take a shot. It goes in!

The coaches have us bring the ball back to the midfield line to kick off again. The other team gets the ball, and a few minutes later, Ana Sofia scores for her team. She is really good!

When our scrimmage is finished, the coaches go over their notes. I watch Coach Belle and keep my fingers crossed that she will choose me. It sure is taking them a long time to decide!

While we wait, my new friends and I sit on the grass in the shade of a big leafy tree, drinking cool water and talking. I find out that Ana Sofia just moved to Jacksonville last year. Her daddy is a doctor, and he got a new job at the hospital. She played on a team where she used to live in Florida. Ava's dad coaches a boys' soccer team and taught her how to play too.

Finally the coaches call us to gather in a circle again. "Thank you all so much for coming today," Coach Kristy says. "Coach Belle and I are going to call out the names of the girls we've chosen for our teams and the positions you'll be playing. When you hear your name, go stand by your new coach."

Coach Belle goes first. "Ana Sofia Garza, midfielder! Ava Randall, defender! Kylie Jean Carter, forward!" she says.

When I hear my name I get so excited, I jump up and down. I forget to listen to the other names, but Coach Kristy must have picked Miranda and Layla because I see them standing by her.

When all of the players are assigned, Coach Belle says, "Congratulations, girls! Let's choose a name for our team."

I raise my hand in the air. "We could be the Tiaras," I suggest.

"How about the Tigers?" Ana Sofia shouts.

"Or the Hurricanes?" Ava adds.

Coach Belle smiles at us. "These are all good suggestions," she says. "I think we should vote. Who wants to be the Tiaras?"

I raise my hand, but no one else does.

"How about the Tigers?" Coach Belle asks. Almost every girl on the team raises her hand.

Coach Belle counts the hands and says, "It looks like we're the Tigers."

I raise my hand again. "Could we add Lilies to our name? Then we could be the Tiger Lilies."

Coach Belle asks, "What do you think, team?"

The girls all cheer.

"That's it then," Coach Belle says. "Go, Tiger Lilies!"

Chapter 4
Practice, Practice, Practice!

The next morning, I can't wait to tell Mr. Jim, my favorite bus driver, my big news! When I get on the bus, I take my favorite seat, right behind him, and tap him on the shoulder.

"Mr. Jim, I have two things to tell you!" I exclaim. "One is exciting and one is important."

Mr. Jim laughs. "You'd best tell me the important stuff first," he says.

"The important thing is that my momma is picking me up after school again today," I tell him. "She is taking me to buy cleats, which are special shoes for soccer players. I need them because I got picked to be a real true soccer player at tryouts yesterday. That's the exciting news! Ta-da!"

"Well, aren't you somethin'," Mr. Jim says. "Congratulations, little gal!"

I grin. When Lucy gets on the bus, I tell her my exciting news too.

Lucy gives me a high five and a hug! "I knew you could do it," she says. "There's no stopping you when you make up your mind about something."

* * *

The rest of the day flies by. I have such exciting news and so many people to tell! Then I meet Momma in the parent pickup line just like I did yesterday.

"Do you want to swing by Bubba Burger first and have a quick after-school snack?" Momma asks me. "It's on the way to the Sports Shack anyway."

"Yes, please!" I exclaim. "That sounds delicious!"

You'll never guess who I see when we get to Bubba Burger — my new friend, Ana Sofia! She is there with her momma too. "Hey, Ana Sofia," I say.

"Hi, Kylie Jean!" Ana Sofia replies with a smile and a wave.

We both step up to the counter and place our order. My favorite thing to get at Bubba Burger is a Jr. Bubba burger meal, but since we're only having a snack, I settle for cheese tater tots and a root beer.

"Why don't we all sit together?" Momma suggests.

I think that is a great idea! We pick a table, and everyone sits down. The mommas have a little chat while we eat. Ana Sofia and I talk about soccer moves.

After we finish our snack, we all head over to the Sports Shack to look for shoes. I am shocked! They don't have very many shoes to choose from, and there are only two color choices: black or white.

I decide to try on the white ones. They're okay, but I sure do wish they could be pink. After all, pink is my favorite color. Just then an idea hits my brain like grass on a soccer ball. I can get pink shoelaces!

"The black ones might be easier to keep clean," Momma suggests.

The salesperson finds a pair of black shoes and even offers to switch the laces out for me. The black shoes and pink laces look so great together. Now I absolutely love them!

I want to wear my new shoes home, but
Momma reminds me that soccer shoes have cleats.
Oh, well. When I get home I can try them on for
Ugly Brother in the backyard.

Back at the house on Peachtree Lane, I meet
Ugly Brother in the backyard. "Do you like my
special new soccer shoes?" I ask him.

"Ruff, ruff, ruff!" he barks in reply.

Two barks means yes, so three barks must
mean he *loves* my new soccer shoes!

"Do you want to help me practice?" I ask him.

"Ruff, ruff!" Ugly Brother barks.

I am not surprised he wants to play. Dogs
just love to play ball, so I bet soccer will be Ugly
Brother's new favorite sport too!

I pass the ball to him, and he stops it with his head. Then he pushes it back to me. He is really good at passing!

When it's time for dinner, I go inside, dribbling the ball down the hallway. While I eat, I pass it between my feet under the table. While I watch my favorite TV show, I try to juggle the ball.

Momma is always telling me that practice makes perfect, and I want to be the best soccer player ever. Luckily, the Tiger Lilies have a practice session the very next day after school!

* * *

The first person I see when I arrive at practice the next afternoon is Ana Sofia. I hurry right over to my new friend. "Are you ready to practice?" she asks.

"Yup!" I say.

First we run drills. When we're done, Coach Belle blows her whistle and tells us, "Time for a scrimmage! Half of you girls will wear black practice jerseys, and the other side can wear white."

Coach Belle hands out the jerseys. I am sad when I see that Ana Sofia is on the black side, and I'm on the white. It is hard to play against your new friend. "I wish I was on your team," I whisper to her.

"Don't worry!" Ana Sofia replies. "Tomorrow is Saturday, and we will both be on the same team as we play our first real true soccer game!"

Chapter 5
Field Time

On Saturday morning I wake up bright and early. It is finally game day! This is no practice scrimmage — today we play against another team, ready or not.

I put on my soccer uniform: shorts, jersey, and socks. As we pile into the van, I see Momma even has her game bag.

When we get to the soccer field, Ana Sofia waves at me. She is wearing the same colorful, stretchy-band bracelets she always wears. I'm so nervous. I sure wish I had some lucky bracelets to wear!

Lots of folks have come to see me play, including my Pappy. I give him a quick wave before the game starts. Pappy loves soccer almost as much as basketball. Momma says he is my number one fan.

"Are you ready?" Ana Sofia asks when I run over to my team.

I nod nervously. "Let's play!"

Ana Sofia gives me a high five. "We are going to rock this game!" she cheers.

We all take our places on the field. We are playing the Wildcats, and some of the girls look a lot older than us. The Tiger Lilies take the kickoff, and I follow the action. Ana Sofia is ruling the midfield. We dribble and pass the ball.

Finally, I see my chance. I kick and score! My fans go wild! I see Pappy on the sidelines whistling and cheering. "Go, Kylie Jean!" he shouts.

I am happier than a coach with a winning team, but not for long. Now the other team has the ball, and they dribble down the field, pressing our defense hard.

One of the other girls fakes a kick and passes the ball to another player who scores! Now we are tied 1-1.

We go back and forth dribbling, both teams stealing the ball. The Wildcats score again with a header, but we quickly catch up with another corner kick. Now the score is 2-2. The game is tied again!

The referee is running up and down the field, following the action. All the fans watch anxiously from the sidelines. Ugly Brother hides his face under his big doggie paws.

I am about to shoot the ball, but just as I pull my leg back to kick it, a bigger player from the other team sneaks in and steals the ball away from me. She quickly dribbles the ball the length of the field and shoots a powerful shot right past our goalie.

Just then, the referee blows the whistle. That means the game is over. We lose to the Wildcats 3-2.

I feel awful. If I play like this, I will never be a great player like Belle Jenkins. Tears sting my eyes, but I'm not gonna cry. Soccer players should be tough.

We line up to congratulate the other team, and when we're done, Coach Belle calls, "Good game, girls! Circle up."

I stand next to Ana Sofia. "Cheer up. You win some games and lose some games," she says. She takes off one of her bracelets and hands it to me. "Here. Wear my bracelet the next time we play, and maybe it will be good luck for you too."

I smile. Ana Sofia is a great friend. "Thanks," I say. "I really want the Tiger Lilies to be winners."

Coach Belle hears me and says, "I do too, Kylie Jean. That's why I'm inviting all of my players to come to a soccer camp next weekend. Please give this flier to your parents, and remember we have a game on Tuesday. See you then!"

All the players shout, "Bye, Coach!" and head off to find our families in the crowd on the sidelines. Momma and Pappy are ready to give me a big squeezy hug. They know I am disappointed.

I give Momma the brochure for the Benbrook Girls' Soccer Camp! It says, "Are you looking for a fun-filled opportunity to develop your skills and get to know the Benbrook Women's Soccer Team? Our two-day camps are for players ages 5-12 who want to work on increasing technical ability in a fun environment with the Benbrook coaches and players."

"Can I pretty please go?" I ask. "Coach Belle invited the whole team."

Momma nods. "Of course you can go," she says. "I wouldn't want you to be the only Tiger Lily who isn't there!"

Chapter 6
Team Spirit

On Monday after school, Ana Sofia comes over to practice. My best cousin Lucy comes over too. Ana Sofia brings a brand-new soccer ball so we can run practice drills. Lucy does not want to play soccer, but she and Ugly Brother chase the ball.

Suddenly an idea hits my brain like a referee on a whistle! "We should play a practice game!" I exclaim. "How about the two of you against Ugly Brother and me?"

Lucy sighs. "What if I don't want to play?"

"Come on!" I beg. "It's just practice. We need your help!"

Finally she agrees. Ana Sofia doesn't know I have a secret weapon — Ugly Brother! He turns out to be a very good player. Lucy is slow and complains a lot, but she did tell us she didn't want to play.

Soon it's time for Ana Sofia to leave. "See you tomorrow at practice," she says.

Lucy's momma comes to get her after supper. Before she leaves I give her a big squeezy hug to say thank you. Even though she didn't want to, she helped us practice. She really is the best cousin in the whole wide world!

* * *

The next day it's time for the Tiger Lilies to play our second game of the season. We all take the field and face off against the Hurricanes. I wear the stretchy bracelet Ana Sofia gave me for good luck.

The Tiger Lilies get off to a strong start when Ana Sofia scores early. We quickly get a second goal from a penalty kick because one of the Hurricane players fouled in the box.

The Hurricanes come back with two quick goals in the second half. They have a really strong forward. She scored both times she touched the ball. For a while the game is at a standstill while we are tied 2-2.

In the last minute of the game, everyone on the sidelines stands up and begins cheering. I see Momma, Daddy, Pappy, Granny, and all my family cheering for me.

With seconds to go, I get the ball and make it all the way down the field, shooting with my left foot and scoring the winning goal! I decide that Ana Sofia's bracelets really are lucky.

The Tiger Lilies show our team spirit, jumping around on the field laughing, hugging, and chanting, "We won! We won!"

Chapter 7
Saturday Soccer Camp, Day One

I am so excited for soccer camp that the rest of the week drags by. But finally the rooster crows, and it is Saturday morning!

I jump right out of bed. The sky is still streaked with light gray wisps from last night, but I'm already awake. I don't want to be late for my first day!

Ugly Brother is up too. He wants to come to camp with me, but no matter how much we beg and plead with Momma, she says, "Dogs are not allowed at camp — even super great soccer-playing dogs."

Momma drives me over to Buccaneer Field and drops me off. First I find Ana Sofia and Ava. It isn't easy! There must be hundreds of girls here! I see lots of coaches too, but luckily I spot Coach Belle right away.

"Circle up, girls!" Coach Belle calls, waving everyone over. "Today we are going to start by practicing the basics of soccer: dribbling, passing and receiving, shooting, and heading the ball. But don't worry, we'll practice these skills in fun competitions."

All the soccer players cheer excitedly. I can't wait to get started!

"Today I want you to focus on your individual skills but also on improving as a team," Coach Belle continues. "It is going to be a fun-filled day of learning, competing, and enjoying soccer!"

I lean over to Ana Sofia and whisper, "I sure am glad we got Coach Belle as our coach. She's the best player around."

Ana Sofia nods in agreement.

Coach Belle breaks all the campers up into groups based on age. Since Ana Sofia and I are the same age, we get to be on the same team! First we warm up, then we work on shooting. This is my best skill.

After we practice for a while, it's snack time. Yum! The sky starts to cloud up as Coach Belle and I stand together on the sidelines and pass out the water and fruit.

I'm so excited to talk to her I forget to talk about soccer! Silly me, I just say, "It looks like it might rain."

"Don't worry too much about that," Coach Belle tells me. "As long as it's not raining too hard and we don't have lightning, we can still keep playing."

After snack time we get back on the field for a shooting competition. That's my time to shine. I make almost all my shots. I am playing like a real true soccer queen!

That afternoon, our lunch is given to us in special soccer-themed lunch bags. We each get a sandwich, chips, and a cookie. Even though it's my favorite, I give Coach Belle my chocolate chip cookie. A few little sprinkles of rain fall while we eat.

Finally we get to play a game against another team, and we win! I'm happier than a goalie blocking a corner shot.

The games are set up like a tournament, so our team gets to play the winning team of another match. Then tomorrow afternoon the two final winning teams will play each other in a championship game!

The sun is peeking out now, and there's not a cloud in the sky, but after playing the first round of games, the field looks like a chocolate mud milkshake. Playing against the next team is not going to be easy.

Our second game is really hard work! During the first half, our goalie seems to anticipate the other team's every move and manges to block all their shots. Our offense is fighting hard to score too, but the other team's defense seems unstoppable.

I want to show everyone that we are champions, and I know I have to make this corner kick count. I race to the top of the box to begin my run. As Ana Sofia kicks the ball, I follow it through the air and jump up for the header. My head connects with the ball, and it flies toward the goal.

At first I'm overjoyed, but then I realize I'm flying through the air too! *CRUNCH!* The ball sails into the back of the net just as I hit the ground hard. We won! My teammates go wild, but I yell, "Oweee!"

I can tell right away that something is really, really wrong. Pain is shooting all up and down through my arm.

Coach Belle immediately dashes onto the field and races toward me. The referee and Coach Kristy come running too, and they all kneel down by my side.

"Someone go get the camp nurse!" Coach Belle shouts over her shoulder to the rest of my teammates. "Run!"

After checking me over gently, the ref turns to
Coach Belle and says, "I think her arm is broken.
She needs to go to the hospital. We'd better call
her parents."

"Don't worry," Coach Belle says after she's called my momma and daddy. "Your parents are on their way. I know it hurts, but it's going to be okay. I had a broken arm a long time ago, and I'm fine now."

But despite what Coach Belle says, I'm scared. I can't stop crying!

Just then, I spot Momma and Daddy running across the field. Daddy scoops me up. "Don't cry, sweet pea," he says. "It's all going to be okay."

Still crying, I ask, "Do I have to go in an ambulance?"

Momma shakes her head. "Nope, we're real close to the hospital, so we'll just go in our van," she tells me.

That makes me feel a little better, but I'm still upset. How am I going to be a soccer queen with a broken arm?

Chapter 8
ER Friends

When we arrive at the hospital, the ER is very busy. Daddy helps me out of the van and carries me inside while Momma follows behind us. Nurses and doctors rush around us as people sit waiting in chairs.

Daddy gets a pillow for me to rest my arm on. "Put your arm on this, princess," he says.

We sit down in the waiting area while Momma fills out lots and lots of papers. "How bad does it hurt if ten means it hurts the most, and zero means it doesn't hurt at all?" she asks me.

"TEN!" I shout.

Momma turns in the forms. Then we have to wait and wait some more. My arm feels like the whole soccer team stepped on it! Finally a nurse calls me back to an examining room, and Daddy lifts me up so I can sit on the table.

After a little while, a doctor in a white coat comes in. "Hi, Kylie Jean," he says. "I'm Dr. Garza."

Wait a minute! He has the same last name as Ana Sofia. And I remember her telling me that her daddy is a doctor — I bet this is him!

"Do you know Ana Sofia Garza?" I ask him.

Dr. Garza smiles. "Yes, I am Ana Sofia's daddy," he says. "And I've heard many stories about you and your famous soccer-playing dog!"

Just thinking about Ugly Brother makes me smile. Too bad dogs can't come to the ER. Ugly Brother always makes me feel better! He would give me doggie kisses or do funny tricks to cheer me up.

"How about letting me ask some questions now?" Dr. Garza says. "How bad is the pain from one to ten?"

"Ten!" I exclaim. "Unless I can say eleven . . ."

Dr. Garza studies my arm and says, "I think your arm is broken, so I'm going to order some X-rays."

I get to ride in a wheelchair to get my X-rays done. If my arm didn't hurt so much, it would really be fun. When we get to the radiology department, lying on the X-ray table is easy, but being still is hard! Then we wait again for the results.

Finally Dr. Garza brings the film in to show us. He points out the different bones in my arm and shows us where the broken one is. It looks just like the arm bone in my game of Operation!

Thinking about that makes me *really* nervous. "Do I have to have surgery?" I blurt out.

Dr. Garza shakes his head. "No. We can just give you some medicine, set the bone, and put a cast on your arm."

"How long will she need to wear the cast?" Momma asks.

"At least six weeks," Dr. Garza replies. "You'll probably be out for the rest of this soccer season."

I start to cry big, sloppy crocodile tears. I can't be a soccer queen from the sidelines!

Momma pats my back and says, "Sweet pea, you can always play next year and every year after that. You can even play in high school and college!"

Momma always knows the right thing to say.

Dr. Garza has some good news for me too. "Did you know you can choose the color of your cast?" he says. "My daughter tells me pink is your favorite color. How would like a pink cast?"

"I wouldn't just like it, I would love it!" I say.

It takes a while, but eventually I have a pink cast on my arm. If you ever have to have a cast, choose pink. It's the best color!

"When I was kid, I broke my ankle," Daddy tells me. "I didn't have a pink cast, but all my friends signed it."

"Maybe all of the Tiger Lilies could sign mine!" I exclaim.

"Maybe Dr. Garza should be the first person to sign your cast," Momma suggests.

"That's a great idea!" I agree. I turn to Dr. Garza. "Would you please sign my cast?"

"Absolutely!" he agrees.

Did you know doctors are very messy writers? I can't even read what he wrote, but Momma says it's just his name.

Chapter 9
Sunday Soccer Camp, Day Two

The next morning, I have a really hard time getting out of bed with my arm in a cast. If you ask me, waking up is hard enough to do with two good arms!

I roll over onto my side, and Ugly Brother pushes me to the edge of the bed. Then I slide over it like a wet noodle.

Once I make it out of bed, I have to figure out how to get dressed for church. I stare into my closet for a few minutes. Finally I decide a sundress will be easiest to put on, so I pick one with pink flowers.

I put it on and look in the mirror. "I guess if I can't be a Tiger Lily, I might as well be a daisy," I tell Ugly Brother.

"Ruff, ruff!" he barks. He thinks that's a good idea too.

I don't have to pack my soccer clothes in my duffel bag to change into after church because there is no soccer for me today. I am sad I'm going to miss the big championship game. Ugly Brother knows I'm feeling blue, so he gives me a big slobbery doggie kiss.

"Are you ready for breakfast?" I ask him.

He barks, "Ruff, ruff."

Ugly Brother carries my shoes downstairs for me. At the breakfast table, Momma has coffee, orange juice, eggs, biscuits, and a big old skillet of sausage gravy ready to eat.

T.J. is loading up his plate, but when he sees me, he offers to fix my plate too!

"Here you go, Lil' Sis," he says, setting it in front of me. T.J. put so much food on my plate that there'll be plenty left to share with Ugly Brother later.

When Momma comes to the table, we all bow our heads to say grace. Then we talk about our plans for after church. Usually we go to Nanny and Pa's farm for Sunday dinner, but today is different. Nanny and Pa have been invited to go out to lunch with their friends, so they're not hosting everyone. This gives me an idea!

"Since we're not going to the farm, we could go to the soccer game!" I suggest.

Momma agrees, but says, "No matter how exciting the game gets, you have to stay on the sidelines with me. Promise?"

"Promise!" I repeat.

Ugly Bother barks, "Ruff, ruff!" I think he wants to go watch the game too!

After church we drop off one brother at home and pick up another. Ugly Brother is very excited, so this time Momma holds onto his leash when we arrive at the park.

We head over to where my teammates are standing. Ana Sofia sees me first and gives me a big squeezy hug.

The rest of the girls crowd in behind Ana Sofia and start asking questions all at once. "Does it hurt? Do you have to sleep in that cast? How long do you have to wear it? Can we sign your cast?"

"Yes, yes, six weeks, and yes!" I reply, answering all their questions at once.

Momma takes a pen out of her game bag. Ana Sofia signs my cast first. She puts her name and under it she writes "Soccer BFFs." The other girls line up to sign it too.

"Did you tell them you wanted a pink cast?" Ava asks.

I wink at Ana Sofia. "That was my doctor's idea," I tell her. "He already knew pink was my best color."

Just then Coach Belle walks up. "I'm so glad to see you here, Kylie Jean. Is there room for me to sign too?" she asks.

"Of course!" I say. "I saved you a spot right by Ana Sofia's name. Thank you for saving me yesterday!"

Coach Belle smiles. "I told you everything would be okay." She signs her name on my cast and then reminds the team it's almost game time.

It's a warm, sunny day, so we find a shady place on the sidelines to cheer on the team. This time Momma sits with Daddy on the ground and I sit on her chair. Ugly Brother sits with me. He is so worried about me that he doesn't even bother running up and down the sidelines following the game's action.

The referee blows the whistle, and the game starts. Right away I can tell that soccer camp has made us better. My teammates are passing right to each other's feet with lightning speed. It's amazing to see!

Unfortunately the other team is moving the ball quickly too. Every time one of my teammates gets the ball, the other team is ready to go in hard for a tackle. They come out strong and score a quick goal before we can gain momentum. Oh, no! The score is now 1-0.

Being behind a point really motivates my teammates, though, and they come back and tie the game five minutes later. Now it's 1-1. I keep shouting and cheering, but the score stays 1-1 for the remainder of the first half.

When the second half starts I just know we're going to score. But both teams are playing a good defense, and no one can get a goal.

"What happens if the teams are tied?" I ask Daddy.

"In a regular soccer game, they would have to play again," he says. "But since it's only camp, I think they'll probably just let it be a tied game."

"Come on, team!" I shout. "You can do it. Score! SCORE!"

With only three minutes left on the clock, Ava manages to steal the ball away from a player on the other team. She immediately passes to Ana Sofia, who is wide open. Ana Sofia takes a quick touch and kicks the ball toward the right corner of the goal.

I hold my breath as the ball sails through the air. Goal! Thanks to Ana Sofia, our team wins! Everyone goes wild! We did it!

Ana Sofia runs over to me on the sidelines and gives me a high five on my uninjured hand. Then the rest of the team runs over to do the same. Even though I couldn't play, I still feel like I'm a part of the team!

Chapter 10
Ice Creams and Big Dreams

To celebrate winning the championship game at camp, Momma takes Ana Sofia and me to the Dairy Bee for ice cream sundaes. It's really busy, and the line is so long it loops around like a wiggly snake.

While we wait, we look at the flavors. They have strawberry, chocolate, marshmallow, pineapple, cherry, caramel, or butterscotch.

When we get to the counter, Ana Sofia and I both pick hot fudge sundaes, and Momma gets a chocolate milkshake. Then we find an empty table by the front window, and Ana Sofia carries our tray over to it.

Scooping up a spoonful, I say, "It's a good thing I didn't break my right arm or eating ice cream would be really hard to do."

"Hey, I just realized something!" Ana Sofia exclaims. "Vanilla ice cream and hot fudge sauce look black and white. We could be eating soccer sundaes!"

"You're right!" I agree with a happy smile. "Speaking of soccer, what was your favorite part of camp?"

"I liked playing the championship game the best!" Ana Sofia replies.

I sigh. "I wish I could have played in that last game."

"If you hadn't gotten that last goal on Saturday, we wouldn't have been playing today at all!" Ana Sofia reminds me. "What was your favorite part of camp?"

I think for a minute, then say, "My favorite part of camp was you, my new best friend!"

I am taking my time eating the rest of my ice cream, but it's starting to melt, so I eat more and talk less until I scoop up the last yummy bite. Then my spoon clangs against the empty sundae glass.

Ana Sofia giggles. "You have a hot fudge mustache!" she says.

Laughing, I wipe it off with a napkin. While she eats the rest of her ice cream, we talk about soccer strategy.

"I'm sad that you won't be able to play any more regular games with the Tiger Lilies," Ana Sofia says.

"Don't be sad. I'll be your number one fan!" I reply. "And even though I can't play this year, I'll be back next year for sure."

My new best friend doesn't know it yet, but she is sitting with a future Benbrook Buccaneer! I have big dreams, and one day I'm going to be real true soccer queen, just you wait and see!

Marci Bales Peschke was born in Indiana, grew up in Florida, and now lives in Texas with her husband, two children, and a feisty black-and-white cat named Phoebe. She loves reading and watching movies.

When **Tuesday Mourning** was a little girl, she knew she wanted to be an artist when she grew up. Now, she is an illustrator who lives in Utah. She especially loves illustrating books for kids and teenagers. When she isn't illustrating, Tuesday loves spending time with her husband, who is an actor, their two sons and one daughter.

Glossary

anticipate (an-TIS-uh-pate)—to expect and be prepared for something to happen

competition (kahm-puh-TISH-uhn)—a contest to see who is the best at something, sometimes done for a prize

drill (DRILL)—a type of training where you practice one specific skill by repeating it

forward (FOR-wurd)—a position in soccer where the person plays near the other team's goal and tries to score

foul (FOUL)—to break the rules in a sport

header (HED-er)—in soccer, when a person hits the ball with his or her head

midfielder (MID-feel-dur)—a position in soccer where the person plays in the center of the field and helps with both offense and defense

motivate (MOH-tuh-vate)—to encourage someone to do something

radiology (ray-dee-OL-uh-jee)—the examining or photographing of bones or organs with x-rays

referee (ref-uh-REE)—the person who supervises a sports match and makes sure the players are following the rules

1. What is your favorite sport? Talk about what makes it fun and interesting.

2. Have you ever been injured and unable to participate in something as a result? What happened? Talk about how it made you feel.

3. Have you ever gone to a sports camp like Kylie Jean? Talk about what you liked and what you didn't like. Would you want to do it again?

Be Creative!

1. At soccer camp, Kylie Jean makes a new friend, Ana Sofia. Write about a time you made a new friend. How did you meet? What did you have in common?

2. Although Lucy isn't that interested in soccer, she and Kylie Jean still have a lot in common. Write a paragraph about something that you and a friend like to do together.

3. Make a get-well card for Kylie Jean. Be sure to decorate it and write something encouraging!

This is the perfect treat for any Soccer Queen! Just make sure to ask a grown-up for help.

Love, Kylie Jean

From Momma's Kitchen

BREATHTAKING BLUEBERRY PANCAKES

YOU NEED:

- 1 1/4 cup flour
- 1/2 tsp. salt
- 1 Tbs. baking powder
- 1 1/4 tsp. sugar
- 1 egg
- 1 cup milk
- 1/2 Tbs. butter, melted

- 1 cup fresh blueberries
- A grown-up helper
- A griddle or frying pan

1. In a large bowl, stir together flour, salt, baking powder, and sugar. In a small bowl, beat together the egg and milk. Add egg and milk into the flour mixture, then add melted butter and gently mix in the blueberries.

2. Ask your grown-up helper to grease a frying pan or griddle. Scoop about 1/4 cup of batter for each pancake onto the griddle. Have your grown-up flip the pancakes when the batter gets bubbly and the edges look firm. Cook until both sides are golden brown. Serve with maple syrup or a dollop of whipped cream for a yummy breakfast treat!

Yum, yum!

THE FUN DOESN'T STOP HERE!

Discover more at www.capstonekids.com

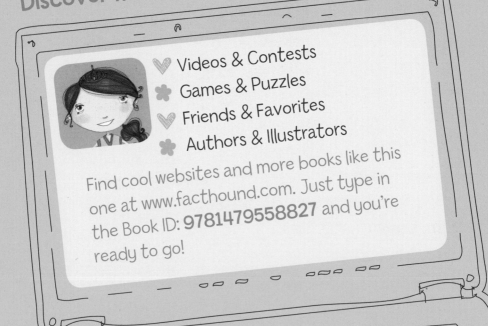

💜 Videos & Contests
❀ Games & Puzzles
💜 Friends & Favorites
❀ Authors & Illustrators

Find cool websites and more books like this one at www.facthound.com. Just type in the Book ID: 9781479558827 and you're ready to go!